The Elves
and the
Shoemaker

Retold by Katie Daynes

Illustrated by
Desideria Guicciardini

Reading Consultant: Alison Kelly
University of Surrey Roehampton

Contents

Chapter 1

Making shoes

Once, an old shoemaker lived
with his wife in a room above
their workshop.

Each day he laid out his leather...

drew different
shoe shapes...

cut them
out...

and sewed
them together.

4

Then he stretched the shoe
shapes over a wooden foot...

cut out more
leather...

and
sewed
it on.

Finally,
he cut out
thick soles...

made holes in
them with a
huge needle...

and sewed the
soles onto
the shoes.

6

People loved watching the
shoemaker at work. Nobody
could go past his workshop
without looking in.

And, at the end of the day,
there was always a crowd of
people wanting to buy his
latest shoes.

Chapter 2

Bad business

One day, the shoemaker's wife spied trouble. A cart passed by the window with **CHEAP SHOES** painted on the side.

At first, she kept quiet. She didn't want to worry her husband. But slowly the crowd outside their workshop became smaller and smaller.

Where is everyone?

I think you should look outside, dear.

A crafty shoe seller had set up a table at the end of their street. His shoes were badly sewn, with poor leather, but he sold them at a bargain price.

Buy your cheap shoes here!

"This is terrible!" said the shoemaker. "He's putting me out of business."

"And his shoes are awful," said the shoemaker's wife.

But the local people were delighted. Now they could buy two pairs of shoes for the price of one.

Each day, the cheap shoe seller arrived with a new load of shoes.

"How can he make them so quickly?" wondered the shoemaker.

He must have lots of people working for him...

Chapter 3

The last
pair of shoes

The next few months were
miserable for the shoemaker
and his wife.

With very little business, they were running out of money. Soon, the shoemaker could only afford enough leather to make one more pair of shoes.

I'm ruined!

He cut out the shoe shapes
and laid them on his work
table. Then he yawned.

"I'm too tired to sew these
today," he sighed.

15

Early next morning, he went downstairs and stopped in amazement.

"Am I still dreaming?" he asked himself.

There on his work table stood a perfect pair of shoes. Someone had neatly sewn up his pieces of leather. What's more, they had sewn shiny buckles on the front. The shoemaker was baffled.

Chapter 4

It must be magic

"They're lovely!" said the shoemaker's wife, putting the shoes in the window. Before long, a rich gentleman came in.

18

"Those shoes are just what I'm looking for!" he cried. "They're much better than the cheap pairs down the road." And he paid for the shoes with a solid gold coin.

Keep the change.

Now, the shoemaker could buy enough leather to make two pairs of shoes.

As he cut them out, he saw how late it was.

"I'll finish them tomorrow," he thought.

But, by morning, the job was already done. Two neat pairs of shoes were waiting for him, fancy bows and all.

That day, the puzzled shoemaker had two more happy customers.

Aren't they gorgeous!

Now, he had enough money to buy leather for four pairs of shoes. After cutting out the leather, the shoemaker locked up and went to bed.

The next morning, he couldn't believe his luck. On the table stood four perfect pairs of shoes.

"It must be magic!" he cried.

Are you sure you locked the door?

And so it went on. The more leather the shoemaker cut, the more shoes he found in the morning.

Chapter 5

The two rivals

Within weeks, business was booming. The shoemaker had plenty of money and very little to do.

He was a happy man. The cheap shoe seller was not so happy. He had angry customers to deal with...

and word had spread about his awful shoes. No one wanted to buy them.

25

One evening, there was a
knock at the shoemaker's door.
It was the shoe seller.

"What can I do for you?"
asked the shoemaker.

"You can stop ruining my
business!" shouted the seller.

He picked up one of the shoemaker's new shoes and studied it carefully.

"And you can give me back my helpers," he snorted.

With a scowl, the shoe seller stormed out of the workshop.

The shoemaker and his wife
looked at each other.

"Who do you think is
making our shoes?" whispered
the shoemaker.

"I don't know," said his wife,
"but let's find out."

Chapter 6

The secret
shoemakers

That night, they decided to
stay awake and see what
happened. They hid behind
some coats in a corner of
the workshop.

Everything was quiet...
until midnight. Two little elves
rushed in, wearing nothing but
rags. They sat down at the
table and quickly began to sew.

The shoemaker and his wife listened carefully to the elves' chatter.

"This is better than making cheap shoes in that rotten attic," said the first elf.

"I wish the other elves had escaped as well," said the second.

"Never mind," replied the first elf. "If we put that wicked shoe seller out of business..."

"...the other elves will be free too!" cried the second.

Hurry up or we'll be spotted.

I'm almost done.

As the sun began to rise,
they finished the last shoe and
disappeared through the door.

The shoemaker and his wife
were astonished.

"I think I'm going crazy,"
said the shoemaker. "Were
those really elves?"

That's
incredible!

His wife nodded. "And it
sounds like that shoe seller is
forcing other elves to work for
him!" she said. "No wonder he
can make so many shoes..."

Chapter 7

Revenge

Over breakfast the next day,
the shoemaker and his wife
discussed how they could help
the elves.

35

By ten o'clock, there was
already a room full of people
wanting to buy the
shoemaker's new shoes.

"If we keep selling these
lovely shoes," said his wife,
"the shoe seller will go bust!"

By midday, they had sold thirty pairs. They were eating lunch when they heard the sound of a cart. The cheap shoe seller was leaving early...

A mob of angry customers were hopping after him, shaking their fists and pelting him with broken shoes.

The shoemaker and his wife breathed a sigh of relief.

"How can we ever thank our two helpers?" wondered the shoemaker.

"Let's make them some proper clothes," said his wife.

Chapter 8

The elves' escape

All day, the shoemaker's wife worked at her sewing machine, making little suits for the elves. The shoemaker made two tiny pairs of shoes.

40

That night, instead of leaving leather shapes on the table, the shoemaker left two piles of clothes.

Then he and his wife hid behind the coats again and waited for the elves to arrive.

The elves were delighted
with their new outfits. They
scrambled into them and
danced around the room.

42

"Here they are!" called a voice from the street.

A second later, there were fourteen more elves in the workshop. The two elves stopped dancing.

"Hey!" said one. "How did you all escape?"

"The shoe seller let us go!"
cried an excited elf. "He's
giving up selling shoes."

We put
spells on our
sewing...

...to make
the shoes fall
apart!

"Now we're going to
celebrate," said another.
"Come on – and you can tell us
why you're dressed like people!"

44

Laughing and joking,
the elves skipped off down
the street.

The shoemaker and
his wife smiled as they
watched them go.

They might have lost their magic helpers, but now they were in business again. They had plenty of customers and lots of ideas for new shoes.

As for the elves, they never sewed another shoe.

About this story

The Elves and the Shoemaker was first written down by two brothers, Jacob and Wilhelm Grimm. They lived in Germany two centuries ago and together they retold hundreds of fairy tales.

Cinderella, *Rapunzel* and *Snow White* are just a few of their other famous stories.

Series editor: Lesley Sims

Designed by
Russell Punter

First published in 2004 by Usborne Publishing Ltd., Usborne House,
83-85 Saffron Hill, London EC1N 8RT, England. www.usborne.com
Copyright © 2004 Usborne Publishing Ltd.